Big Dog and Little Dog

Dav Pilkey

Houghton Mifflin Harcourt

Boston New York

Copyright © 1997 by Dav Pilkey

Activities © 2015 by Houghton Mifflin Harcourt

For information about permission to reproduce selections from this book,

write to Permissions, Houghton Mifflin Harcourt Publishing Company,

215 Park Avenue South, New York, New York 10003.

Green Light Readers® and its logos are trademarks of HMH Publishers LLC,

registered in the United States and other countries.

www.hmhco.com

Library of Congress Cataloging-in-Publication Data is on file.

ISBN 978-0-544-43070-9 paper-over-board

ISBN 978-0-544-43069-3 paperback

Manufactured in China

SCP 10 9 8 7 6 5 4 3 2 1

4500521215

Ages	Grades	Guided Reading Level	Reading Recovery Level	Lexile® Level
4–6	K	D	5–6	240L

To Eamon Hoyt Johnston

Big Dog and Little Dog are hungry.

Big Dog and Little Dog want food.

Here is some food for Big Dog.

Big Dog is happy.

Here is some food for Little Dog.

Little Dog is happy, too.

Big Dog and Little Dog are full.

Big Dog and Little Dog are sleepy.

Big Dog gets in the big bed.

Little Dog gets in the little bed.

Big Dog is lonely.

Little Dog is lonely, too.

Shhh.

Big Dog and Little Dog are sleeping.

🐾 Picture It 🐾

Read the sentences below.
Which picture matches each sentence?

Big Dog and Little Dog are sleeping.

Here is some food for Little Dog.

Little Dog is sleepy.

Little Dog is lonely in his little bed.

 Hot Dog!

Can you believe these dog facts?

🐾 The Beatles song "A Day in the Life" includes a high-pitched whistle that only dogs can hear.

🐾 In ancient China, an emperor often kept a small Pekingese dog hidden up his sleeve for protection.

🐾 When Lord Byron was told his dog could not come with him to Cambridge Trinity College, he brought a bear instead.

🐾 Dogs sweat from their paws—on really hot days they leave wet footprints!

🐾 In 2003, Dr. Roger Mugford invented the "wagometer," a device that explains a dog's exact mood by measuring the wag of its tail.

**The story of Big Dog and Little Dog got scrambled!
Can you put the scenes in the right order?**

A

B

C

D

E

 Dog-Libs

Learning Nouns and Verbs

Ask a friend to make a list of seven nouns and five verbs. One verb should end in "-ed" and one verb should end in "s." Use the words to complete the story. Does your friend know how to take care of a dog?

Noun - a person, place, or thing
Verb - an action

Caring for a dog is fun, but it's a lot of

(noun) ! You must (verb) and (verb)

and (verb) a dog. They should be fed

healthy (noun) — no (noun) , (noun) ,

or (noun) . After dinner, they need to be

(verb, ending in —ed) . If they get dirty they need

a (noun) . This may seem like a lot of

(noun) , but it's worth it when your

dog (verb, ending in s) your face.